Juv
794.7
Om 6
2016

FOND DU LAC
PUBLIC LIBRARY
NOV 13 2015
WITHDRAWN
RECEIVED

D1788537

Wild Stunts
INCREDIBLE CAR STUNTS

by Tyler Omoth

Edge Books are published by Capstone Press,
1710 Roe Crest Drive, North Mankato, Minnesota 56003
www.capstonepub.com

Copyright © 2016 by Capstone Press, a Capstone imprint. All rights reserved. No part of this publication may be reproduced in whole or in part, or stored in a retrieval system, or transmitted in any form or by any means, electronic, mechanical, photocopying, recording, or otherwise, without written permission of the publisher.

Library of Congress Cataloging-in-Publication Data
Cataloging-in-publication information is on file with the Library of Congress.
ISBN 978-1-4914-4254-8 (library binding)
ISBN 978-1-4914-4315-6 (eBook PDF)

Editorial Credits
Nate LeBoutillier, editor; Kyle Grenz, designer; Jo Miller, media researcher; Tori Abraham, production specialist

Photo Credits
Alamy: Lightworks Media, 12, Moviestore Collection Ltd, 18-19, Powerhouse, 11, RIA Novosti, 14; Getty Images: Chicago History Museum, 20, The Enthusiast Network/Fred Enke, 17 (inset), Richard Bord, 28-29; ISC Archives via Getty Images, 7; Newscom: akg-images, 6, Itar-Tass Photos/Savintsev Fyodor, 4-5, Kent Homer/Invision for Mattel/AP Images Supplied by WENN.com, 22-23, UPI/Teresa Prentice, 26, WENN Photos, 21, WENN Photos/Rui M Leal, 9; Rex USA, 8; Shutterstock/Tatiana Belova, cover; The Kobal Collection: 20TH CENTURY FOX, 18, CBS-TV, 16, DANJAQ/EON/UA, 24-25

Design Elements
Shutterstock: antishock, Eneng Lindawati, Igorsky, Leigh Prather, Radoman Durkovic

Direct Quotations
Page 8, from October 15, 2013, *Sunset Gun* post "The Roaring Road to Ruin: Wallace Reid" by Kim Morgan, www.sunsetgun.typepad.com.
Page 17, from March 15, 2014, *Los Angeles Times* article "'Need for Speed' director Scott Waugh's need for reality" by Richard Verrier, www.articles.latimes.com.
Page 19, from December 15, 1997, Welcome to Silent Movies post "Speeding Sweethearts, Part I" by William M. Drew, www.welcometosilentmovies.com.

Printed in the United States of America in North Mankato, Minnesota.
032015   008823CGF15

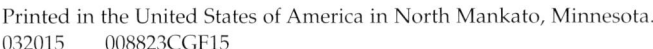

Table of Contents

Ready to Go **4**

Pushing the Limits **6**

**Elements of the
Car Stunt** **10**

**Stuntmen and Stuntwomen
of Note** **16**

The Wildest Car Stunts **24**

Glossary **30**
Read More **31**
Internet Sites **31**
Index **32**

Ready to Go

Strapped in and ready to go, you stare through the windshield of your highly specialized car. The road before you leads to the stunt you've been waiting to pull off. The engine idles. Your body tingles with excitement and fear. The stunt has been researched and approved for safety. But there is still an element of danger.

You inch the car forward gently and take a deep breath. As you pick up speed, you hit the gas and give it all the car has to give. You approach a ramp, and then you launch. In mid-air everything is quiet. You're flying! You soar over flaming boxes, or other cars, or water. You land with a jolt and slow up. As quickly as it starts, it's over. You did it! You are an incredible stunt driver.

Car and driver pull off a fiery stunt at the Prometheus Festival of Stunt Art in Moscow, Russia.

Pushing the Limits

The Car Comes to Life

In 1886 German Karl Benz patented the first gasoline-powered automobile. It was a mechanical marvel that could move people and cargo from place to place without using horses. However, it was quite slow and difficult to *maneuver* with just three wheels. Within five years Benz upgraded his design to make a four-wheeled car that greatly improved the machine's stability. As cars became more powerful, faster, and safer, the limits to what they could do also expanded.

Karl Benz with his wife Berta in 1894

maneuver—a planned and controlled movement that requires practiced skills

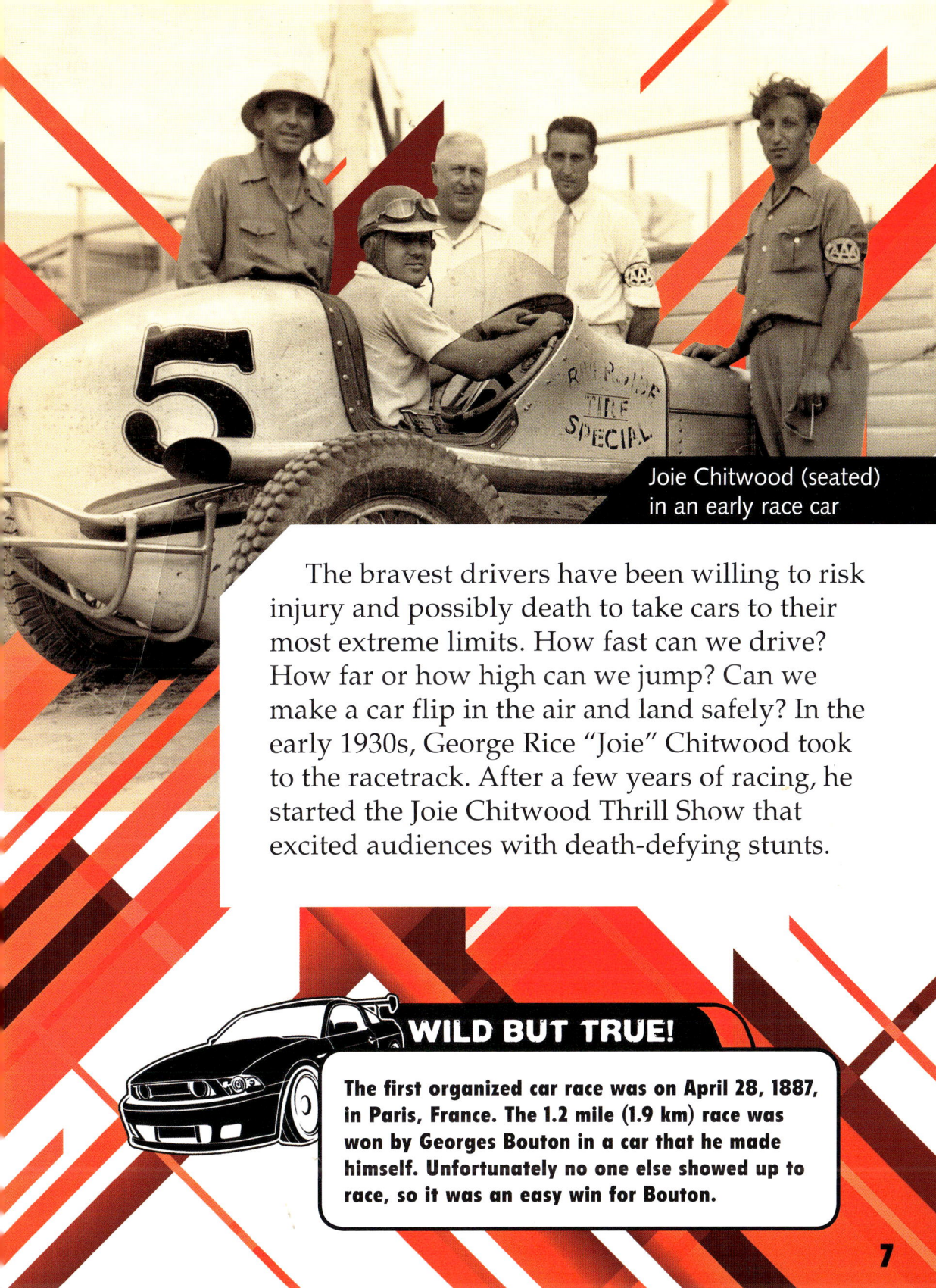

Joie Chitwood (seated) in an early race car

The bravest drivers have been willing to risk injury and possibly death to take cars to their most extreme limits. How fast can we drive? How far or how high can we jump? Can we make a car flip in the air and land safely? In the early 1930s, George Rice "Joie" Chitwood took to the racetrack. After a few years of racing, he started the Joie Chitwood Thrill Show that excited audiences with death-defying stunts.

WILD BUT TRUE!

The first organized car race was on April 28, 1887, in Paris, France. The 1.2 mile (1.9 km) race was won by Georges Bouton in a car that he made himself. Unfortunately no one else showed up to race, so it was an easy win for Bouton.

Daredevils Behind the Wheel

The early 1900s was the era of silent movies. Wallace Reid was a popular actor whose good looks and charm made him a favorite on the silver screen. When Reid wasn't acting, he was driving or working on cars. He brought his love of driving to the film world. He starred in *The Roaring Road* in 1919 and *Double Speed* and *Excuse My Dust* in 1920. These action-packed movies showcased grand car chases and wild racing scenes.

> "Whether speeding down an open road or through the air, I feel a surge of blood through my veins that prompts me to ever-increasing speeds."
> **Wallace Reid**

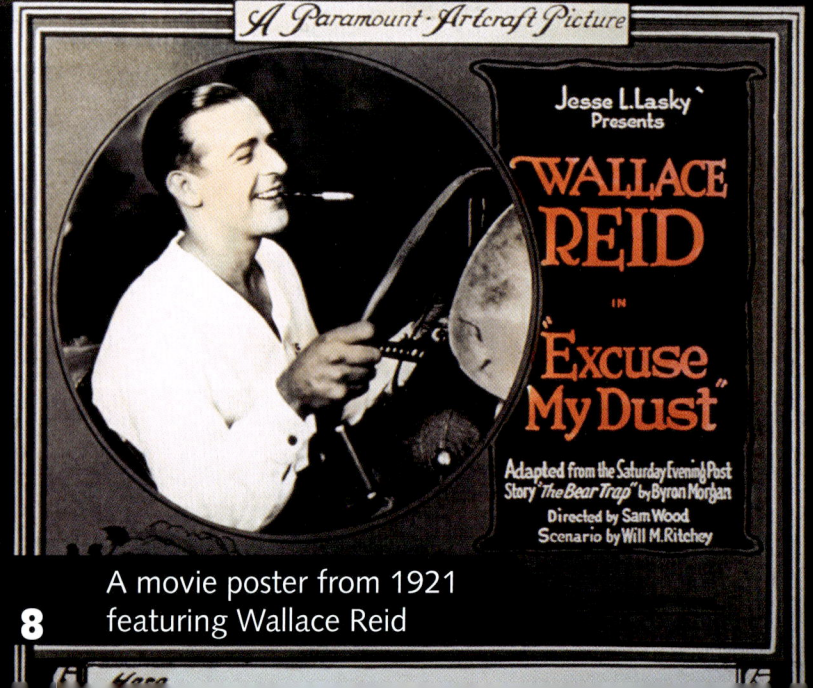

A movie poster from 1921 featuring Wallace Reid

CHECK THIS OUT! The Ford Model T was first made available in 1908. The earliest models had top speeds of 40–45 miles (64–72 km) per hour.

Pioneers such as Reid set the stage for other stuntmen to test the limits of cars. British driver Terry Grant was born in 1970 and began driving at the age of six. Driving around his family's farm, he discovered that he had talent. Grant now holds many Guinness World Records for stunt driving, including the fastest one-mile (1.6 kilometers) time for driving in reverse. In 2013 he set the record for circular "donut" spins, pulling off 39 donuts in 100 seconds.

pioneer—a person who is the first to try something new

Elements of the Car Stunt

The Evolution of Car Stunts

There were only a few types of cars in the early 1900s. As more and more models were created, the desire to compare them grew. What better way to compare two cars than to race them? Over time cars grew faster and more powerful. Naturally, drivers longed to see just what else these new machines could do.

Early cars were very heavy. They didn't go too fast. But drivers worked with what they had. They learned how to maneuver wheels in order to make cars do extraordinary things. Today's cars are lighter, faster, and better *engineered* for stunt driving than ever before. That means that today's stunts are also bigger and better.

CHECK THIS OUT! The first seat belt was invented by English engineer George Cayley in the late 1800s.

engineer—to make something happen by using a scientific plan

An early car jumps over a "fallen bridge" in a promotional stunt from the 1920s.

Ramping It Up

Drivers need special equipment to push the limits of stunt driving. Some of the first stunts were jumps. To get cars *airborne*, cars need lift. To get lift, cars use ramps. Ramps come in a variety of sizes and shapes to help drivers create astonishing stunts. Some ramps are very large in order to help launch cars into long or very high jumps. Other ramps are small and help drivers get the car up on two wheels. For jumps that include spinning or flipping the car, ramps need to be specially designed using very precise *calculations*. With the right ramp and the right speed, drivers can pull off thrilling stunts.

Drivers need a place to perform their stunts. Special tracks that are in isolated environments help keep both the drivers and spectators safe. Stunts should never be attempted on public roads.

airborne—carried by the air; in flight

calculation—use of a mathematical process to determine an outcome

WILD BUT TRUE!

The the best-selling driving video game series is *Need for Speed*. From 1994 to 2014, the popular game sold nearly 100 million copies.

Alexei Latotsky performs a flaming car stunt.

Preparing For the Worst

It is no secret that car stunts are dangerous. High speeds, crash landings, and sudden stops are all a part of stunt driving. Rollovers, crashes, and crash landings occur even when car stunts go according to plan. It's important that drivers protect themselves with safety precautions.

All stunt drivers wear protective helmets when doing stunts. Seatbelts that are specially made keep them strapped in even if their cars roll over. Their suits are made of special materials that protect them in case fire breaks out.

The cars are also specially made with safety in mind. They have strong brakes so they can stop quickly. They also have extra strong *shock absorbers* to soften the impact of landing jumps. The frames of the cars are usually *reinforced*. This helps to maintain the car's shape in a crash and protect the driver inside.

CHECK THIS OUT! Stunt driver Hal Needham claims that he has broken as many as 56 bones in his body doing stunts.

shock absorber—a device on a vehicle that lessens the shock of driving on rough surfaces

reinforce—to strengthen the structure or shape of something

Stuntmen and Stuntwomen of Note

Carey Loftin began his stunt-driving career in the 1930s. He became known as a legendary Hollywood stunt man. By the 1960s he was sought after for the most challenging chase scenes and stunts. Loftin was a driver for *The Dukes of Hazzard*, a TV showed that aired from 1979–1985 and was known for its chases and wild jumps. His chase scene in 1968's *Bullitt* with Steve McQueen is considered one of the best in movie history.

When the director of 1984's *Against All Odds* needed a stunt man for a thrilling Ferrari chase scene, he turned to Loftin. Even though Loftin was 68 years old by that time, he was still considered the best in the business. Loftin was a rare stuntman who avoided serious injury throughout most of his career. He worked as a stunt driver for more than 60 years with 195 stunt credits to his name.

WILD BUT TRUE!

Carey Loftin was hired to work on the set of the 1990 film, *The Rookie* with Clint Eastwood. Well into his 70s by then, Loftin was hired mainly to share stories of his greatest stunts to the film's cast and crew.

Carey Loftin

CHECK THIS OUT! *The Dukes of Hazzard* featured an orange Dodge Charger named The General Lee. *Dukes* stunt drivers wrecked more than 300 General Lees in seven years.

With the right car and a dare, modern stunt drivers are ready for anything.

Bill Hickman made a career in the movies, mostly behind the wheel. Hickman's work in the 1971 movie *The French Connection* is considered **legendary**. In that movie, one memorable scene features a car wildly chasing an elevated train.

Scott Waugh watched his dad do stunts and grabbed the wheel for a 20-year career as a stunt man. In 2014 he directed the film *The Need for Speed*, which included many dramatic chase scenes.

Travis Pastrana is fearless. He drives in NASCAR races and holds the record for longest jump by a rally car. He has also won several X Games medals and gained fame for his **motocross** feats.

Experts plan a stunt for the 1973 movie *The Seven*.

"We went back out on the road, traveling at high speeds and hanging out the side of the car to film this. I wanted the audiences to really feel what it's like to drive 230 miles [370 km] per hour."
Scott Waugh, on filming *The Need for Speed*

A stunt scene from the 2014 movie *The Need for Speed*.

legendary—remarkable enough to be well-known or famous
motocross—a sport in which people race motorcycles on dirt tracks

Move over guys—there are plenty of women who want to take the wheel. From the beginning of the automobile, women have also been fascinated with cars.

In 1916 actress Gloria Swanson was hooked after her first driving lesson. She went on to star in films like *The Danger Girl* and *Sunset Boulevard* that featured her in cars.

"I turned out to be a natural [driver]. I quickly learned to wheel around in tight circles, go into instant reverse, and take bumps and curves."
Gloria Swanson

Gloria Swanson

Georgia Durante's first appearances on TV were as a model. Durante learned how to drive early in life. Somehow she briefly got caught up working as a getaway driver for members of the mob. She turned that into a career as a stunt driver in movies and television shows and commercials, mostly in the 1990s.

Georgia Durante

Sera Trimble got her start as a valet in Seattle. When a director saw her park a car while driving very fast, he nudged her into a career as a stunt driver. Trimble has driven in car ads as well as on the set of the TV show *Hawaii Five-O*.

The Wildest Car Stunts

Some stunts have been done over and over again. Others are so daring and so imaginative that they never lose their wow factor.

The Double Loop Track

Just like on a Hot Wheels toy track, Tanner Foust and Greg Tracy drove their life-sized Hot Wheels cars through a fully-looped track. That means that at one point their cars were actually upside down. While this stunt did not require extreme speeds, there was a lot of danger involved.

Back Flip

The back flip is a stunt that has been tried many times unsuccessfully. But in 2013, French stunt driver Guerlain Chicherit pulled it off in spectacular fashion. Driving a modified Mini Countryman car, Chicherit sped off of a specially designed ramp. Then he completed a 360-degree backflip in mid-air before landing on a 26-foot (7.9 meter) high snow ramp. The snow softened the landing, giving this amazing stunt a perfect ending.

CHECK THIS OUT! In 2013 Hot Wheels attempted a single-car, double-loop stunt with a *drone* car, but it crashed.

drone—an unmanned, remote-controlled aircraft

Stunts On the Silver Screen

James Bond films are known for their crazy stunts. For the 1974 film *The Man with the Golden Gun,* stunt driver Lauren "Bumps" Willert pulled off an amazing feat. Willert made the first ever filmed *barrel roll* jump by hitting a corkscrewed ramp and jumping over a river. This stunt was years ahead of its time and made for one fantastic scene.

barrel roll—a type of inversion in which a vehicle turns in a circle sideways

CHECK THIS OUT! The car used in the barrel roll stunt from *The Man with the Golden Gun* was a 1974 AMC Hornet X Hatchback.

In 2005's *Batman Begins*, stunt man George Cottle raced Batman's Tumbler vehicle through the streets of Gotham, which was actually Chicago. Multiple versions of the Tumbler were created—one with a real jet engine on the real fueled by six propane tanks. The moviemakers wanted to film the action scenes with the Tumbler. They were going for a realistic, rather than digital, effect. Cottle could not see out of the windshield, so he had to rely on TV monitors inside the vehicle.

Jumping, Sliding, and Spinning into the Record Books

Once someone has done a stunt, someone else wants to beat it. These drivers aren't afraid to attempt the impossible.

Tanner Foust sets the distance jump on May 29, 2011 in Indianapolis, Indiana.

Distance Jump Record

Tanner Foust is a rally car driver and X Games champion. He was the first car driver to do a full loop. He also holds the record for the longest jump by a four-wheeled vehicle of 332 feet (101 m).

Tight Parking Spot

In November of 2014, Chinese stunt driver Han Yue set the world *drift* parking record. Speeding towards a parking spot that was just 3.15 inches (8 centimeters) longer than his Mini Cooper, Yue pulled the brake and slid the car sideways right into the spot.

drift—a controlled power slide that happens around a curve

Longest Distance on Two Wheels

In 2009 Italian driver Michele Pilia drove his specially modified BMW car on just two wheels for 230.57 miles (371.07 km). By driving just one side of the car off of a small ramp, he was able to pop it up on two wheels. Keeping the car balanced for so long required intense concentration and skill. The car's modifications redistributed the weight of the car to help it balance.

Guerlain Chicherit makes his world-record attempt on March 18, 2014.

Longest Car Jump In Reverse

In 2014 driver Rob Dyrdek launched his Chevrolet Sonic RS an amazing 89 feet, 3.25 inches (27.21 m) through the air while driving in reverse. He had to drive backwards very fast, hit the ramp, and land safely on the opposite ramp to complete the record. He spun out on the landing and ran the car into a protective wall but was not hurt. Dyrdek does reality TV stunts and is also a professional skateboarder.

CHECK THIS OUT! French driver Guerlain Chicherit attempted to break Tanner Foust's long distance jump record in 2014. Unfortunately, his 360-foot (110-m) attempt ended in a fiery wreck. Luckily, Chicherit did survive.

Glossary

airborne (AHR-bohrn)—carried by the air; in flight

barrel roll (BAYR-uhl ROL)—a type of inversion in which a vehicle turns in a circle sideways

calculation (kal-kyuh-LEY-shuhn)—use of a mathematical process to determine an outcome

drift (DRIFT)—a controlled power slide that happens around a curve

drone (DROHN)—an unmanned, remote-controlled aircraft

engineer (en-juh-NEER)—to make something happen by using a scientific plan

legendary (LEJ-uhnd-air-ee)—remarkable enough to be well-known or famous

maneuver (muh-NOO-ver)—a planned and controlled movement that requires practiced skills

motocross (MOH-toh-kross)—a sport in which people race motorcycles on dirt tracks

pioneer (pye-uh-NEER)—a person who is the first to try something new

reinforce (ree-in-FORSS)—to strengthen the structure or shape of something

shock absorber (SHAHK ab-SORB-uhr)—a device on a vehicle that lessens the shock of driving on rough surfaces

Read More

Catel, Patrick. *Surviving Stunts and Other Amazing Feats.* Extreme Survival. Chicago: Raintree, 2011.

Goldsworthy, Steve. *A Daredevil's Guide to Stunts.* Daredevils' Guides. North Mankato, Minn.: Capstone Press, 2013

Wood, Alix. *Stunt Performer*. The World's Coolest Jobs. New York: PowerKids Press, 2014.

Internet Sites

FactHound offers a safe, fun way to find Internet sites related to this book. All of the sites on FactHound have been researched by our staff.

Here's all you do:

Visit *www.facthound.com*

Type in this code: 9781491442548

 Check out projects, games and lots more at *www.capstonekids.com*

Index

Benz, Karl, 6
Bouton, Georges, 7

Cayley, George, 10
Chicherit, Guerlain, 22, 29
Chitwood, George Rice "Joie," 7
Cottle, George, 25

Dukes of Hazzard, The, 13, 16
Durante, Georgia, 21
Dyrdek, Rob, 29

Eastwood, Clint, 17

Foust, Tanner, 22, 26

Grant, Terry, 9
Guinness World Records, 9

Hickman, Bill, 18
Hot Wheels, 22, 23

Loftin, Carey, 16, 17

McQueen, Steve, 16

Pastrana, Travis, 18
Pilia, Michele, 28

Reid, Wallace, 8

safety equipment
    helmets, 15
    seatbelts, 10, 15
    suits, 15
Swanson, Gloria, 20

Tracy, Greg, 22
Trimble, Sera, 21
types of cars
    AMC Hornet X, 25
    Chevrolet Sonic RS, 29
    Dodge Charger, 13
    Ford Model T, 9
    Mini Cooper, 27
    Mini Countryman, 22

Waugh, Scott, 18, 19
Willert, Lauren "Bumps," 24
world drift parking record, 27

Yue, Han, 27

X Games, 18, 26